THE MOZART MYSTERY

LOL Detective Club Book #4

By E.M. FINN

THE MOZART MYSTERY: LOL DETECTIVE CLUB, BOOK 4

First Edition, August 2016

Cover Illustration by Steven Bybyk and Natalie Khmelovska
Cover Design by E.M. Finn

Table of Contents

CHAPTER ONE

"Salzburg, Austria, here we come!"

Lottie opened her map of Europe and traced her finger across the countries until she landed on Austria, the small country next to Germany and Switzerland.

Their train sped towards the tiny town of Salzburg, Austria. Salzburg was the birthplace of Wolfgang Amadeus Mozart, one of the most famous musical composers of all time. Ollie and his identical twin sisters, Lottie and Lucy, stared out the window as the old city came into view.

"Are we really going to get to see where Mozart was born?" Lucy asked.

"That's what Dad says."

Ollie pointed to their dad, who was asleep in the seat in the next row. Lottie, Ollie, and Lucy Parker traveled the world with their father, Justin Parker, who was a photographer for an important magazine. This time, they were visiting Salzburg, a small European city in the country of Austria. Mozart was born there over two hundred years ago.

"I wonder what kind of cool stuff they have at the Mozart Museum," Ollie said.

"I don't know. But, I heard that Mozart's violin is inside his childhood bedroom. Someone famous is going to play it while we're visiting," Lottie said matter-of-factly.

"Where did you hear that?" Ollie asked.

"From the newspaper, of course," Lucy said.

Lucy loved to read more than anything else in the world. She read everything she could get her hands on. Lucy opened the newspaper that was laying across the seat in the aisle next to her and began reading aloud.

"On January 27th, the Mozart Museum will host a birthday party for the composer at his childhood home. Hans Avery, the famous violinist, will be performing on Mozart's childhood violin."

"January 27th? That's tomorrow," Lottie exclaimed.

"It sure is," Lucy said. "It says here that the violin has been locked inside a glass case for many years. Tomorrow will be the first time it's been taken out for someone to play."

"Wait a minute. A birthday party? How old is Mozart turning, anyway?" Lottie asked.

"Lottie, Mozart died a long time ago. He was born in 1756, over two hundred fifty years ago! I think the birthday party is in his honor."

"Oh," Lottie said quietly. "Still, it sounds like a lot of fun!"

In the next row, their dad opened his eyes and stretched his arms sleepily.

"We're almost there," their dad said as he looked out the window. "We're going to the Mozart Museum first. I need to get some things set up for my photo shoot tomorrow. After that, we can head over to the hotel. Thankfully, it's right around the corner from the Museum," Dad smiled.

"Cool!" Lucy and Lottie said at the same time. They loved staying in new hotels, especially historic ones in old European cities.

"Guess I'd better do some reading about Mozart's hometown," Lucy said as she dug into her bag and pulled out her travel book about Austria.

Lottie scooted close to her twin sister and read the book over her shoulder. The two girls looked exactly the same, right down to their dark hair and big brown eyes. They looked so much alike, even their dad had a hard time telling them apart.

Lucy stuck her nose into the book and read aloud:

"It says here that the first musical instrument Mozart learned to play was the clavier. He was only three years old when he started learning music."

"What's a clavier?" Ollie asked.

"It was an instrument like the piano," Lucy said.

"Wow, Mozart played the piano just like me," Lottie exclaimed. Lottie had just started piano lessons back home and loved to play the piano every chance she got.

Lucy looked at her twin sister for a minute before she spoke.

"Well, not exactly. Mozart was composing symphonies by the time he was our age," Lucy said. "He loved to play music with his older sister, who he called Nanerrl. Her real name was Maria Anna, but Mozart never called her that."

"Kind of like how you call me Lottie, even though my name is Charlotte," Lottie said.

"Exactly," Lucy smiled.

Just then, the train lurched to a stop at the Salzburg Station. The kids grabbed their bags and hopped out into the busy train station. The station was huge and looked like something out of a movie. They passed a gift shop on the way out of the train station. The gift shop was filled with lots of cool gadgets and souvenirs from Austria.

"Look at all this fun stuff," Lottie said as she sifted through a bin in the gift shop doorway. She picked up a small remote control clicker and pushed a button. Several lamps in the store all turned off at once. Smiling, she clicked the remote control again, and the lamps turned back on. "Awesome!"

the front door.

"This is so cool!" Ollie exclaimed as he took out his tablet to take a picture.

"I can't wait to see what's inside the museum," Lucy said.

"I think whatever's inside, it must be delicious," Lottie said as she sniffed the air. "And good thing, because I'm hungry from all that traveling."

"Lottie, I think that yummy smell is coming from the pastry shop next door. Austrians are known for their amazing desserts. If you're hungry, I bet we could grab a strudel there later," Lucy said.

"What's strudel?" Lottie asked.

"It's a delicious fruit filled dessert they make in Austria. You'll love it," Lucy said.

"I bet I will," Lottie giggled. "Let's see inside the museum first."

CHAPTER TWO

The kids walked through the thick oak front doorway of the Mozart Museum, and climbed the stairs up to the third floor. Mozart's apartment was larger than it appeared from the outside, with rooms that echoed and creaky old wood floors. Snowflakes flurried outside the big window, as fresh white snow blanketed the street below.

"Where is everyone today?" Lucy asked as she glanced around the empty room.

"Today is Sunday so the museum is closed," Dad said. "But I need to come and scout the place to get set up for taking pictures tomorrow. I need to make sure that everything is just perfect when I photograph Hans Avery at the birthday party."

"Hans Avery? Who's that?" Lottie said.

"He's the famous violinist who's going to be playing Mozart's violin," Lucy said.

"You guys take a look around, but be careful and don't touch anything. Everything in this house is the same as it was when Mozart lived here over 250 years ago," Dad said.

The kids walked from room to room in the house. Glass cases holding sheet music, paintings, and other artifacts lined the curved walls. It had a very clean, empty feel, like a museum. Finally, they arrived at Mozart's bedroom, which was decorated with furniture from the 1700s. A wooden bookcase sat in the corner, filled with crusty old books. A fancy grand piano sat in the center of the room. The windows had heavy drapes that were pulled open to let the daylight inside.

Near the window was a small violin, hanging in mid-air, locked inside a thick glass case. Lucy looked at it carefully. It was a beautiful and very old looking, with darker staining around the edges of the wood. She could see red lasers pointing at the violin from inside the case.

"I wonder what those lasers around the violin do?" she said.

"They keep out the thieves," Ollie said. "If anyone tries to break into that case to steal the violin, the alarms would go off. It's a priceless violin, so they have to keep it safe."

Lottie wandered around the room, looking at the furniture and at the simple art hanging on the walls. She walked up to the piano. It was dark black with an ornate top. The keys on the piano were yellow and looked very old.

"I wonder if Mozart played on this piano,"

Lottie said dreamily.

"I bet he did!" Ollie said. "He might have even composed some of his most famous works on it."

Just then, a loud musical sound rattled the once silent room.

"What was that?" Lucy exclaimed.

Lucy looked over and saw Lottie leaning against the piano. Lottie's arm was touching one of the keys.

"Lottie! Remember what dad said about touching things," Lucy exclaimed.

"Oh right. Sorry!" Lottie said sheepishly. "It was an accident. I got lost dreaming about what it would have been like to meet Mozart."

The kids walked around the empty room while Ollie made a movie on his tablet.

"What are you recording?" Lucy asked.

"I want to post this video up on my blog for my friends back home to see," Ollie said. "No one is going to believe that we actually got to hang out at Mozart's house."

The kids walked over to the house's kitchen. It was an authentic kitchen from back in the 1700s, with no refrigerator or modern stove in sight. Over by a round wood kitchen table, a tall woman with dark black hair was putting pastries on a silver platter.

Lottie got a gleam in her eye as she eyed the gorgeous chocolate pastry puffs. When the woman turned away, Lottie reached her hand onto the silver tray without asking.

"Lottie!" Ollie said quickly. Lottie looked up at her big brother and then at the pastry chef. Her face turned red with embarrassment.

"I'm so sorry. They just looked so delicious. I couldn't help myself," Lottie apologized.

"Go ahead, take one," the woman said. "But first, you have to introduce yourself."

"Thank you, ma'am. My name is Lottie, and this is my twin sister Lucy and my big brother, Ollie. We're visiting the museum with our dad.

He's here to photograph the birthday party for Mozart."

"You're Justin Parker's kids?" the woman said. "I met your dad earlier. He's such a nice man."

She reached out her hand to shake the kids' hands.

"I'm Greta Galley and I own the pastry shop next door. We have a big event coming up tomorrow with the birthday party, so I'm getting all the desserts ready ahead of time."

"Will there be birthday cake at the party?" Lottie asked.

"Of course! What's a birthday party without birthday cake? And music, too. I hear that they're going to take Mozart's violin out of its glass case so that Hans Avery, the famous violinist, can play a song on it," Greta said excitedly. "Which song do you think Mr. Avery will play?" Greta asked the kids.

"Maybe Happy Birthday to Mozart," Lottie

said.

"Or maybe one of Mozart's songs he composed on that violin," Lucy said matter-of-factly.

The kids heard footsteps approaching and looked up to see their dad standing in the doorway to the kitchen. He had his coat and scarf on, and looked like he was ready to head back outside into the cold.

"I see you've met my kids, Greta. I hope they've been on their best behavior," he said.

"Oh, they have!" Greta smiled. "I hope to see you kids again at the birthday party tomorrow. I'll even save you guys each a slice of birthday cake."

"You've got it," the kids said at the same time.

"Guys, I've finished setting up for tomorrow. What do you say we get out of here and explore the city while we've still got some daylight?" their dad said as they walked downstairs and out of the museum.

CHAPTER THREE

Snow fell down on the street in heavy flakes. The kids stared at it through the windows of the first floor lobby. They bundled up in their coats and scarves, and put on their gloves.

"I've never seen so much snow. Can we go skiing?" Lottie asked. In the distance, she could see the snow-capped mountain range.

"I'm afraid we don't have time for skiing to-day," Dad said. "But we could go find some hot chocolate. I hear that Salzburg has some of the best hot chocolate in Europe."

"I read that they put raw eggs into their hot chocolate," Ollie said. "Is that true?"

"Very true. I read it in my book," Lucy added.

Suddenly, their dad's cell phone rang out loudly. He answered, and after a few moments, hung up the phone and gave the kids a worried look.

"Guys, I'm afraid I need to have a meeting with my editor. You go ahead and I'll meet you back later at the hotel. Stick together and don't get into any trouble."

"Sure thing, Dad," Ollie said.

The kids walked out the front door of the museum and onto the snowy cobblestone street. As soon as they opened the door, they were immediately hit with an icy blast of cold air. Just then, the door of the pastry shop beside them opened and a warm gust smelling of cinnamon wafted out onto the street.

CHAPTER FOUR

The kids woke up the next morning to a flurry of snow outside their hotel room window.

"Time to bundle up," Ollie said as he slid on his puffed up parka coat. The coat was filled with goose feathers and was almost as big as Ollie.

"You look like a marshmallow," Lottie chuckled.

"Well, then you do, too," he said as he looked at his sister in the mirror. They both had on white puffy ski jackets that blended in with the white snow that blanketed the street.

They walked down the snowy path towards the Mozart Museum, their footprints making fresh tracks in the falling snow.

By the time they got inside the museum, it was packed with people ready for the birthday party. They made their way back up to Mozart's bedroom, where the violin was kept. The bedroom was very crowded, and it was hard to hear over the voices of the guests talking. The room was brightly lit by a simple crystal chandelier overhead. The heavy blue curtains in the room were closed, which made the lighting even more dramatic.

"It's almost time," a man with a mustache announced.

"Who's that?" Ollie asked.

"Oh, that's Bert Berry. He's the director of the Mozart Museum. He's going to be the one to take Mozart's violin out of the glass security

24

case today," Lottie said.

"Wow, how did you know that, Lottie?" Ollie said.

Lottie pointed to a sign over the door. "It says right there on the birthday party schedule. At noon, Bert Berry will be presenting the violin to Hans Avery to play."

"Oh, I see it now," Ollie laughed.

Bert Berry cleared his throat and brought the room to attention.

"My dear fellow Mozart fans. Over two hundred fifty years ago, our beloved Mozart was born in this very bedroom. He played this violin as a boy, and composed some of the world's most beloved pieces on this magnificent instrument. Today, we will hear the brilliant music of Mozart played by the amazing violinist, Hans Avery," Bert Berry said in a thick Austrian accent.

The crowd clapped loudly, and the kids could hardly hear what Bert Berry was saying.

A short, plump man with flushed red cheeks stood next to Mr. Berry.

"I recognize him from the posters down on the street. That's Hans Avery," Ollie whispered.

Hans Avery fidgeted nervously as he looked around at the crowd of people. After a moment, the Museum's director spoke again.

"Without further ado, let's unveil the world-famous and one-of-a-kind violin," Bert Berry said as he cleared his throat.

Mr. Berry took a long silver key and pushed it gently into the bottom of the glass box. An electronic keypad with green lights popped up and Mr. Berry punched in a secret code.

"There we have it," he said nervously.

Just as the door to the violin case opened, all the lights in the room went out. The room was suddenly pitch black. The crowd began talking excitedly, and it was hard to hear a thing.

"Who turned off the lights?" A woman screamed over the noise.

It was so dark in the room, no one could see a thing. After a moment, the lights came back on as if nothing had happened.

The kids glanced around the room, but everything looked the same. Bert Berry cleared his throat nervously.

"No need to worry, folks. All is well. It was probably just the snow storm causing a brief electrical outage," he said.

After the room had quieted down, Bert Berry took a moment to finish his speech.

"As I was saying, this one-of-a kind violin was played by Mozart when he was a young child, touring Europe and playing for Kings and Queens. We will now hear one of Mozart's sonatinas on the violin, played by the world-renowned violinist, Mr. Hans Avery."

But, before Mr. Berry handed the violin to Mr. Avery, Lucy yelled out across the crowd.

"Stop! That's not Mozart's violin. It's a fake!"

CHAPTER FIVE

"A fake? You can't be serious," Bert Berry said. The crowd in the room murmured uncomfortably, and people gave each other confused looks.

"I am serious," Lucy said. "I noticed yesterday that the original Mozart violin had a scratch at the bottom. But, this violin doesn't have any scratches at all."

"How could the violin be a fake? It's been in the same glass case for many years," Mr. Berry said as he looked suspiciously at Lucy.

"Well, I'm sure," Lucy said confidently.

Dad walked over and patted Lucy on the shoulder. "Are you sure about that, sweetie? I don't see how the violin could be a fake. It was in that glass case with all those alarms and lasers."

Lucy nodded her head. She stared at the violin and wanted to reach out to touch it, but thought better of it.

Mr. Berry examined the violin from top to bottom. He looked at the wood neck of the instrument. He plucked the strings and listened to the tone.

"Goodness, I think the girl is right. This violin is a forgery. Why didn't I notice that before?" Mr. Berry said as he played with his gray mustache.

"But we saw the real one yesterday. When could the switch have happened?" Ollie wondered.

"The violin is watched by guards at night. An alarm will sound if the case is opened. And, as you could see, the case had not been opened," Mr. Berry said quietly.

"The glass case wasn't opened last night, Mr. Berry. It was opened just now. When the lights went off," Lottie said.

"Oh my, you're right!" Mr. Berry exclaimed.

"Seal the doors," Lucy commanded. "The violin is in here somewhere, and the LOL Detective Club is on the case."

"The LOL Detective Club?" Mr. Berry said as he gave Lucy a funny look.

"It's the name of our mystery solving team. LOL stands for Lucy, Ollie, and Lottie," Lucy smiled.

"Or Lottie, Ollie, and Lucy," Lottie shot back.

"We've been solving mysteries all over the world. And we've never lost a case," Ollie added.

"Wonderful. You guys start peeking around, and in the meantime, I'll call the police at once," Mr. Berry said.

"Oh, that's not necessary, is it?" Hans Avery said. "We can search everyone as they leave. Surely, if nobody has the violin on them, then they are free to go. It's a small violin – but not so small you could stuff it into your pocket," Hans said.

Mr. Berry scratched his head as he looked at the violin.

"Fine. But, I want to call in an expert to examine the violin. I'm still not convinced the violin is a fake. I'm not sure I believe the opinion of an eight-year-old American girl," he frowned as he looked at Lucy.

A crowd started to form around Mr. Berry and the violin.

"I'm sorry, friends, but the birthday celebration is cancelled," Mr. Berry said. "We'll have the party another day." Everyone groaned.

The museum guests formed a line out the front door, as the museum security guards checked their pockets and coats for a sign of the violin. Not one person had the violin in their coat.

"Now that everyone else is gone, the real detective work can begin," Lucy said.

CHAPTER SIX

A few minutes later, a woman arrived. She was short and round, with white hair that that curled around the base of her neck. She wore a red coat with large buttons and had a brightly colored hat and gloves that were dusted with a thin layer of snow.

"I'm Petra Sands," the woman said. "I'm an expert in all things Mozart, and a frequent guest of the museum. If anyone would know if this violin is a forgery, it would be me. I'm sorry

I wasn't at the party this morning. I had other plans," she said.

"Thank you so much for coming," Mr. Berry said. "We'll have a look at the violin."

Petra examined the violin from top to bottom as Lucy watched from a distance. Petra scribbled a few notes on her notepad and took measurements with a small ruler she pulled from her briefcase.

"Mmmm. Very interesting," she said under her breath.

"What is it?" Ollie asked.

Petra turned to Mr. Berry and handed him the violin. "It's a fake, alright. A real forgery. It's almost correct, but there is no wearing at the base of the violin." She pointed along the bottom lip of the violin. "See, the original would have markings here from age and use."

"Just as I said!" Lucy exclaimed.

"I see," Mr. Berry said sadly. "Thank you for your time, Ms. Sands." He nodded and shook her hand as she left the museum.

As Mr. Berry showed Petra Sands the door, Ollie, Lottie, and Lucy huddled near the piano trying to piece together the few clues they had about the fake violin.

"I wonder if someone had a key to the room?" Lottie said.

"Good point, Lottie. Let me ask Mr. Berry," Lucy said.

Once Petra Sands had left, Lucy walked over to Mr. Berry. He was standing by the dark curtains looking out at the snow falling outside.

"Excuse me, Mr. Berry. I was wondering if you could tell me a few things. I'd really like to help solve this case."

"Of course," Mr. Berry said. "I'd do anything to find the real violin. It's a national treasure."

"We were wondering who has a key to the building?" Lucy asked.

Mr. Berry scratched his head and thought aloud.

"Well, I have a key to the building. And I loan out keys from time to time to employees and workers," he said. "Besides myself, the only person who has a key right now is Greta Galley, the pastry chef from next door. I gave her a key because she was setting up for the birthday party last night. I left before she did and asked her to lock up."

Lucy thought for a minute.

"Greta Galley? No, it couldn't possibly be her, could it?" Lucy said to herself. "She was so nice."

Ollie paced in front of the window. Suddenly, his hand shot up in the air like he'd just had a brilliant idea.

"Wait a minute, guys. I think I've figured it out. All we need to do is check the violin for fingerprints," he said excitedly.

"What do you mean, Ollie?" Lucy asked.

"Well, the original violin has been in a sealed in a glass case for decades. It probably still has Mozart's fingerprints on it," Ollie explained.

"That' so cool," Lottie said. "But, I don't see how that helps us solve the case."

Ollie paced back and forth. "Think about it. The new violin won't have Mozart's fingerprints on it, but it will have someone else's fingerprints. It will have the thief's fingerprints," he said. "All we have to do is hand the fake violin over to the police, and they can track down the forger by the fingerprints!"

"That's a brilliant idea," Lottie squealed. "I'm so glad you're my big brother."

"Not so fast, guys," Lucy said thoughtfully. "I bet whoever switched Mozart's violin for the fake wore gloves. He wouldn't have wanted to risk getting caught."

"He or she," Lottie said. "We don't know if the crook is a boy or a girl."

"Good point," Ollie said. "It could be anyone."

"Anyone wearing gloves, that is!" Lucy said.

CHAPTER SEVEN

Four police cars sped up in front of the museum with their sirens blaring. The officers jumped out, dressed in dark navy blue uniforms with black caps, and formed a line in front of the door.

"I appreciate the LOL Detective Club working on the case," Mr. Berry said to the kids. "But, you'll have to understand that I had to call the police. Now that we know for sure that the violin is a forgery, the clock is ticking to find the thief before they get away for good."

Lottie, Ollie, and Lucy nodded their heads in agreement.

"Don't worry," Lucy said. "We're still working on the case. We'll let the police know when we solve it."

A tall police officer with a wide smile walked up to Mr. Berry. "I'm Officer Wolf, and I'll be handling the investigation," he said.

"Thank you for coming, Officer Wolf. I'll fill you in on the details as soon as we get inside," Mr. Berry said.

"That won't be necessary. We'd like to ask you some questions down at the police station. It's more official that way," Officer Wolf said.

"Of course," Mr. Berry said. "I'm happy to do whatever I can do to help the police find the criminal."

"Wonderful," Officer Wolf said. "And please bring the fake violin. We will need to submit it into evidence."

"Of course," Mr. Berry said.

"I'll come down to the police station with you, Mr. Berry," their dad said. "I'll take some photographs for the magazine. I'm sure my editor will want a story on Mozart's missing violin. What an exciting trip this is turning out to be."

Mr. Berry and Officer Wolf looked crossly at Mr. Parker. They were not amused by his tone.

"Excuse me. What I meant to say is that this is very serious and I do hope we find the real violin soon," Mr. Parker added sheepishly.

"Now, if everyone will please come outside," Officer Wolf said. "I'll have the police lock up the building behind us."

The kids shuffled outside with Mr. Berry and their dad as Officer Wolf locked up the front door of the museum. The snow flurried outside, and fell on the kids' freckled cheeks.

"Lucy, it looks like you have white freckles

instead of brown," Lottie laughed.

"You, too!" Lucy said.

As Mr. Parker started to climb into the police car, Ollie tapped him on the shoulder.

"Dad, would you mind if we stayed here while you're down at the police station? Lottie's pretty hungry, so we'd like to go next door for more of that strudel. Don't worry, we won't wander far."

"Good idea, Ollie," their dad said. "Besides, the hotel is right around the corner. Stick together and try not to get into any trouble," he said with a twinkle in his eye.

As the door to the police car closed, Lucy saw the sad look on Mr. Berry's face.

"Don't worry. Remember, the LOL Detective Club is on the case," Lucy whispered.

Mr. Berry smiled weakly as the kids waved goodbye.

As soon as the police car was out of sight, Lottie spun around in the freshly laid snow.

"All this detective work is really making me hungry!" she said.

"Hungry? We've barely even started working on the case," Lucy laughed at her. "But still, some apple strudel does sound nice."

"Besides, maybe some good food will warm us up and help us think about what to do next," Ollie said as he shivered on the sidewalk.

The kids headed right next door to Greta's bakery. The snow stopped falling, and the entire street was blanketed in a white coat of snow.

"It's like a winter wonderland," Lucy marveled.

"I feel like I'm walking on clouds," Lottie said. "I could float away!"

"If only we had some skis," Ollie said. "Can you imagine how fun this would be?"

The kids walked into the warm bakery. Wood logs burned in the fireplace in the corner of the cozy room. The kids scooted a table near the fire and warmed themselves. Outside the window, the scenery looked like the inside of a snow globe.

Greta Galley carried over a tray of different kinds of strudel for the kids.

"A real Austrian sampler. I hope you like it."

Lottie's eyes got big. "What's not to like? I'll take an apple filled one, please."

"They're all for you guys. I have so many left over from the party," Greta said. "I couldn't believe that Mozart's violin was stolen. What did the police say? Do they have a suspect yet?"

"Not yet, but we're on the case," Lucy said. "We'll have the thief figured out in no time."

Lottie took a bite of her apple strudel. Lucy looked up and noticed that Greta's face was red, and she had sweat beading on her forehead. She looked nervous.

"Are you okay?" Lucy asked. "You look like you might be sick."

"I'm fine," Greta said quickly. "It's just hot

next to the stove. I've been baking since yesterday. Maybe I need a little fresh air."

As soon as Greta left, the kids bunched up together and began to whisper.

"That was strange. Do you think she took the violin? She looked awfully guilty," Ollie whispered.

"I don't know," Lucy said. "Why would she do a thing like that?"

"Well, that violin is worth a lot of money. I bet she could sell it and then she could expand her bakery," Ollie said. "What do you think, Lottie?"

Lottie was looking around the corners of the room, lost in a beautiful daydream.

"Earth to Lottie. Are you listening?" Ollie said.

"Oh, sorry. I was just wondering if Mozart ate strudel at this same table when he was a kid. Maybe he even wrote his compositions here," she said dreamily.

"Lottie, I don't think there was a bakery here way back then," Lucy laughed.

"Why not? Didn't they have strudel when Mozart was alive?"

The kids giggled and ate the strudels until they were too stuffed to take another bite. After a moment, Lottie got up from the table and stretched.

"I'm going to ask Greta if she has any more of that Almdudler drink. I'm so thirsty, I could pop!"

"I can't believe you have any more room in your stomach. If I drink that soda pop, I will pop," Lucy giggled.

Lottie wandered towards the back of the bakery, and looked into the kitchen. Greta Galley was nowhere in sight. Lottie kept walking through the back hallway until she'd reached the alley behind the bakery.

"Ms. Galley, are you out here?" Lottie called.

Just then, Lottie saw Greta Galley unlock the back door of the Mozart Museum with her key. Greta slipped inside the museum and disappeared up the back steps.

Lottie threw her hands over her mouth in shock. She raced back to the table where Ollie and Lucy were cleaning up their plates.

"Guys! I just saw Greta Galley sneak inside the museum!" Lottie exclaimed.

"What?" Ollie said. "Why didn't you follow her?"

"By myself? What if she locked me up there?" Lottie said. "Dad told us to stick together, remember?"

"Since when do you listen to Dad?" Ollie joked.

"Seriously, Ollie! We don't have time to argue," Lucy said. "Let's follow Greta and find out what she's up to!"

The kids tossed their trash into the waste basket and crept to the back of the café, into the alley.

"What could she possibly be doing inside the Mozart Museum?" Lucy whispered. "Doesn't she know it's a crime scene now?"

"We're going to have to follow her and make sure she doesn't see us," Ollie said. "That's the only way we'll know for sure what she's up to."

As they walked towards the backdoor of the museum, it swung open and Greta Galley walked out with something hidden under her apron.

The kids dove behind a dumpster, careful that she didn't see them hiding.

"Phew! That was close!" Lottie said. "What do you think she has under her apron?"

"I bet she has Mozart's violin," Ollie said. "She probably hid it and ran back upstairs to find it."

Greta walked past the dumpster and back inside the bakery. After a moment, the kids heard her calling for them from inside the café.

"Lottie, Ollie, Lucy?" Greta called. "Are you guys still here? You left something at the table," she said.

"Oh no, I left my backpack at the table," Lottie said.

"It's okay, Lottie. We need an excuse to talk to Greta to see what she's hiding. We should go back," Lucy said.

"I'm too nervous to talk to her," Lottie said as her lip trembled. "What if she really is the thief? Who knows what she'll do to us."

"We'll stick together, and if anything seems weird, we'll run," said Lucy. "We can do this!"

Ollie's lips were turning blue from the cold as the girls talked.

"Guys, I don't want to rush you, but it's awfully cold out here. I might freeze solid before you decide what to do. I'm about to turn into an ice sculpture."

"Fine, Ollie. Let's go ask her some questions. Don't worry, guys, I'll do the talking,"

Lucy said.

The kids went back inside the café and Lucy grabbed her backpack.

"Ms. Galley? Are you still here?" Lucy called.

But, the café was empty and the front door was locked. Greta Galley had left without a trace.

CHAPTER EIGHT

The kids were silent as they stood in the empty bakery. Finally, Ollie said what they'd all been thinking.

"We need to go back inside the Mozart Museum. I bet there's a clue inside that will help us solve the case. We'll be able to figure out if it was Greta Galley who switched the violins," Ollie said.

"There's got to be a clue somewhere inside," Lucy agreed.

The kids walked out the back door of the bakery and into the empty alley. They followed Greta Galley's footprints in the snow to the backdoor of the Museum.

"Guys, the backdoor is open. Greta forgot to lock it when she left," Ollie said.

"Oh, good," Lottie sighed.

Lucy hesitated. "Wait, do you think that means we're walking into a trap?" she said.

Ollie scratched his forehead. "I guess we're about to find out!"

Greta's snowy footprints led them all the way up the three flights of stairs, until they were standing outside the door to Mozart's bedroom. Ollie pushed the door and it creaked open. They were alone inside the big, dark room. The curtains were closed, making the room almost pitch black. In the dark, the room was completely empty and a little spooky.

"It's so dark in here. I'll open the curtains," Lottie said as she walked towards the drapes.

"No!" Ollie and Lucy shouted at the same time.

"We don't want anyone down on the street to see us snooping around," Lucy said. "Remember, we're on a secret mission."

"Right. I'll find the light switch. It's got to be around here somewhere," Ollie said as he stumbled through the dark room. Ollie felt his way through the darkness over to the wall and found the switch. It was a very fancy, high-tech switch, and it took him a few moments figure out how to turn on the lights.

Lucy and Lottie both squinted as their eyes adjusted to the bright light.

"The room looks exactly the same to me," Lottie said. "What are we looking for?"

"Clues, of course. And who knows, maybe the violin is hidden somewhere inside this room," Lucy answered. She began to search around the room, looking underneath the furniture for any sign of the violin.

Lottie walked over to Mozart's bed and sat down on the edge. After a minute, she relaxed on the mattress, her head hitting the soft pillow.

"Not as comfortable as the hotel bed, but it'll do," she said dreamily.

"Lottie! What are you doing? You can't sleep on Mozart's bed," Lucy said quickly.

Lottie yawned. "But, I want to take a nap. All those strudels made me sleepy," Lottie yawned.

Lucy gave her sister a stern look.

"Okay. I'm getting up," Lottie said. "Tell me where to start looking."

"Just search for what's different," Lucy said. "There's got to be a clue in here to help us solve the case!"

The kids searched all around the room, but they couldn't find anything that looked different. Ollie walked over to the window and peeked through the heavy curtains at the street down below. The snow had started to pick up and their icy footprints were now hidden by a fresh dusting of snow.

"Think, Lucy, think!" Lucy said to herself as she paced the room.

Lucy walked over to the bookshelf in the corner of the room. On the shelf were books about Mozart and his childhood in Salzburg, Austria. The books looked new and they didn't fit with the centuries old décor of the bedroom.

"I wonder what these books are doing in here?" Lucy whispered. She picked up one of the books off the shelf, and the bookcase opened to a secret room.

"Guys, you'll never believe it! It's a secret door," Lucy said excitedly.

Lottie and Ollie ran over to Lucy and peeked inside the secret room hidden behind the bookshelf.

"It looks like some kind of a closet," Ollie said.

They pushed the bookcase through to the other side and saw a small hidden room. It had some empty boxes in the corner, and a round window that looked out onto the street below.

Just then, the sound of Mozart's ghost whooshed past them.

"Hey, that's the same sound we heard at the Greta's bakery!" Ollie said.

The noise grew louder. Lottie put her hands over her ears to keep out the noise.

"Guys, look. It's the window. It's open a crack," Lucy said.

Lucy pushed the window closed, and the noise stopped completely.

"That noise wasn't Mozart's ghost at all," Ollie said. "It was the wind coming through the crack in the window."

Ollie opened the window a little, and the noise started again. He closed it and the noise stopped.

"See?" he said.

"That's one mystery solved," Lucy beamed. "Now we just have to solve the case of Mozart's violin."

CHAPTER NINE

The kids walked out of the hidden office and back into Mozart's bedroom. They looked at the empty glass case where the violin was usually kept. All three of them had frustrated expressions of their faces.

"Mr. Berry brought the fake violin down to the police station. The case looks so empty now," Lottie said.

"Guys, I think we should give up. We've searched everywhere, and there's no sign of the real violin or any clues," Ollie said.

"Let's focus, guys. I know we're missing something," Lucy said. "We've just got to figure out what it is." Lucy thought for a moment as she paced the floor.

"Wait a minute," Ollie said. "Do you remember how I filmed this room yesterday for my blog? The footage is still on my tablet. I bet if we look at the video, we might find a clue."

"That's a great idea, Ollie," Lucy squealed.

Ollie took his tablet out of his backpack and selected the video from yesterday. It showed the kids in the room, as Lottie and Lucy walked around looking at all the artifacts in Mozart's bedroom. The video walked past the bed, the violin, and the grand piano.

"Wait! Scroll it back," Lucy said excitedly.

"What is it?" Lottie asked.

"Right there. Do you see the difference? Yesterday the top to the piano was open and today it's closed."

Lottie sat down at the piano and tried to play it. The notes sounded strange, like the hammers inside the instrument weren't firing.

"Guys, the piano doesn't even work," Lottie said. "How did Mozart compose his music on a broken piano?"

"Wait a minute," Ollie said. "Keep playing, Lottie."

"But you said we're not supposed to touch Mozart's stuff," Lottie said.

"This is an emergency," Ollie said.

Lottie played the song she'd learned at piano lessons, but she could hardly hear the notes.

"There it is. Do you hear that rattling sound?" Ollie said. "I think there's something inside the piano!"

"What do you mean?" Lottie said as she stopped playing. "I think it just sounds that way because it's old."

Lucy walked over to the piano. "No, I think Ollie's right. We've got to open the piano up and see what's inside."

Lottie and Ollie both looked at her wide-eyed.

"Open it up?" Lottie said. "What if we break it?"

"We'll be careful," Lucy said. "It's the only way to know for sure."

Lucy carefully opened up the top of the piano and Ollie used his tablet to shine a light inside the instrument. Dust flew out of the piano in puffy clouds.

Lottie coughed. "That dust is making me sneeze. Achoo!" she said as she sneezed right on the piano keys.

"That's incredible!" Ollie shouted.

"What, Ollie? It was just a sneeze!" Lottie laughed.

"No, look inside!" Ollie said. Lucy and Lottie peered inside the piano. Mozart's violin sat resting upon the dusty springs.

"Look, the violin has scratches around the

bottom, just like Mozart's violin does. It must be the real thing."

"No wonder the piano sounded funny," Ollie said. "The piano hammers were hitting the violin instead of the strings."

"How did Mozart's violin end up inside the piano?" Lottie asked.

"The thief must have hidden it in there," Lucy said.

"My guess is that when the lights in the room went out, somebody grabbed Mozart's violin out of the case, and put it inside the piano. Then, the thief replaced it with the fake violin before the lights were turned back on."

"Why would anyone go to all that trouble just for an old violin?" Lottie asked.

"Whoever the thief was must know how much Mozart's violin is worth," Ollie said.

"No, I meant why did he put the violin inside the piano? That seems like a funny place to hide something." Lottie frowned.

"I bet he needed a place to store the violin so the police wouldn't catch him. He's probably planning on coming back for it later," Ollie said.

"He or she," Lottie corrected him.

"What?" Ollie gave Lottie a puzzled look.

"We still don't know if the thief was a man or a woman," Lottie said smartly.

"That's true," Ollie said sheepishly. "Looks like the case is solved. We found the violin."

"It's only half-solved. We have to find out who did it and make sure that it doesn't happen again," Lucy said.

Lucy stared at Ollie's tablet for a moment. "Wait a minute. Ollie, did you record any video today at the birthday party?"

"Of course I did. I have everything up until the lights went off," Ollie said.

"We have to watch it. I bet we can see the thief in the video. It had to be somebody in the room," Lucy said excitedly.

"How can you be sure?" Lottie asked.

"We can see when the lid on the piano was closed. That will tell us exactly when the violin was stolen. If we can see who is next to the case when that happens, I bet we can figure out who switched the violins!"

"Why didn't I think of that before?" Ollie laughed.

Ollie turned on his tablet and started scrolling through the video from earlier in the day. At first, it was just a bunch of random footage of people walking around talking. Nothing seemed out of the ordinary.

"Wait, stop right there," Lucy said.

"What do you see?" Ollie asked.

"At the beginning of the day, the top to the piano was open. So, now we have to figure out when the piano top was closed," Lottie said.

The piano stayed in the shot as Ollie scrolled further into the video.

"Okay, here is the part when Bert Berry

opened up the violin case with his key. The case is opened and then boom, the lights go out. That's when I turned off my tablet," Ollie said.

"Why did you do that?!" Lucy said.

"I got nervous, I guess," Ollie blushed.

"Let's look at the facts. We know the piano top was open until the lights went out. Then, the thief put the violin inside the piano and shut the top before the lights came back on. By the time the lights came back on, the violins had already been switched." Lucy said.

"That's a lot of quick thinking," Ollie said. "But, wouldn't we have heard the piano top opening and closing?"

"No way. It was so loud in the room when the lights went out. Remember how that one lady screamed?" Lottie said.

"Yea, I thought she was an opera singer," Ollie laughed.

"Or a strangled cat," Lottie chuckled.

CHAPTER TEN

"Let's look to see who is standing next to the violin when the glass case is opened. It has to be someone close enough to grab it and make a quick switch," Ollie said.

The kids looked through the video, searching for the thief.

"The thief could be anyone. There were so many people at the birthday party. It will be impossible to narrow it down to one person," Lucy said.

"What about Greta Galley?" Lottie said. "Where's she in the video?"

Ollie scrolled back through the video.

"Greta Galley was in the back of the room when the lights went off. Look, she's setting up the table where she was going to put the birthday cake," Ollie said.

Lottie turned around and looked towards the back of Mozart's bedroom where the table from earlier in the day was still set up.

"Maybe Greta came back to get her silver platter." Lottie pointed to the video. "Look, in the video the silver platter was there on the table and now, it's gone!"

"That would explain things," Lucy smiled. "But if it isn't Greta Galley, who could it be?"

Ollie rewound the video one last time. In the video, almost everyone in the room had taken off their heavy winter coats, as the heat in the room made it quite warm. Everyone except Hans Avery. He was still wearing his long, wool coat. His face was red and beaded with sweat. His legs poked out like sausages from the bottom of his coat.

"Hans Avery's coat looks big enough to hide a violin inside. Don't you think?" Lucy said.

"Yes, nobody would've checked his coat before the violin was stolen. And he knew exactly what the real violin looked like," Ollie added. "It would have been easy for Mr. Avery to make a fake."

"And look at the bulge in his coat pocket. It's big enough for a violin," Lucy said. "What if he had the violin inside his coat and switched the violins once Mr. Berry opened the glass case? When it was dark, no one would have been able to see him do it."

"If he did it, he was fast. The lights were off only for a few seconds," Lottie said.

All of a sudden, they heard a creak on the back stairwell and footsteps approaching.

"Guys! Someone is coming. What if it's the

thief?!" Lucy whispered.

A shadowy figure crept up the stairs towards them. The footsteps were heavy on the old wooden stairs. Before Lottie could scream, Lucy threw her hands over her sister's mouth.

"Don't make a sound," Lucy whispered. She grabbed Mozart's violin and clutched it close to her chest. "The thief's going to have to deal with me if he wants this violin," she said.

"No time for that, Lucy. We've got to hide!" Ollie said.

Ollie pointed to the bookcase that had the secret room behind it. He grabbed Lucy and Lottie's hands and dashed inside the secret room just in time. The kids held their breaths, trying not to make a sound. Lottie's lip started to tremble and she looked like she might burst into tears.

"Stay calm," Lucy whispered. "Remember, we're in this together."

Ollie peered out from the small crack behind

the bookcase. He saw a short, plump man with red cheeks walking around Mozart's bedroom.

"Guys, it's Hans Avery!" Ollie whispered.

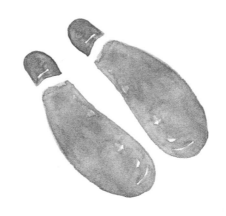

CHAPTER ELEVEN

Hans Avery, the famous violinist, glanced around the room and crept towards the grand piano. He lifted the antique top of the instrument. It made a loud creak as he pushed it open.

Ollie watched everything from the crack in the secret door. Lucy held Mozart's violin carefully on her lap and squeezed Lottie's hand for comfort.

"What's he doing?" Lucy whispered to Ollie.

"Shhh," Ollie whispered. "I'll tell you in a minute."

Hans searched inside the piano for the violin. But, of course, it was not there. It was safely on Lucy's lap in the hidden closet. Hans' eyebrows began to sweat and his face turned so green it was almost purple.

"I know it's here somewhere," he said.

He closed the piano top and started searching frantically around the room. He came dangerously close to the bookcase with the hidden door.

The kids huddled close together in the small hidden room. Lottie fidgeted, trying to hold still as she started to shake nervously. As Lottie shifted to steady herself, her knee brushed the violin on accident. Musical notes from the violin rang out over the once silent room.

"Who's there?" Hans whispered hoarsely. "That sounded like E, A, D, and G. I've been playing the violin all my life. I know the sounds of the strings well."

Hans walked towards the bookshelf, to the spot where the violin had made the noise. He examined the bookcase, and saw a small crack in between the bookshelf and the wall.

"Clever," he said.

Hans pushed hard on the bookcase to try to open the secret door, but it was stuck.

"We've got to get out of here," Ollie whispered.

Ollie tiptoed over to the small round window in the room and opened it all the way. He looked down to the ground. It was three stories down to the street.

"That's way too far to jump!" Lottie whispered.

"But look, there's a fire escape," Lucy said.

Just below the window, there was a long metal ladder that led down to the street below.

"We can climb out the window if we hurry," Ollie whispered.

Hans continued to push on the bookcase, trying every possible way to pry it open. The kids climbed through the window one by one. It was a tight squeeze and they nearly got stuck as they pushed through the small opening. Lucy was the last to leave. Her head dipped under the window and out of sight. She closed the window behind her just as Hans pushed open the bookcase door to the secret room.

"That was close!" Ollie whispered as he hung on tightly to the fire escape ladder. One by one, the kids climbed down the ladder to the alley. Lucy held the violin under her arm as she climbed down one-handed.

"Be careful, Lucy," Lottie whispered. "That's a priceless treasure you're holding with your armpit."

"Thanks, Lottie," Lucy laughed nervously.

Just as they reached the ground, they saw Greta Galley throwing trash into the dumpster in the alley.

"What are you kids doing climbing down the fire escape?" she asked.

"We found the violin thief! He's inside the museum. Lock the door while I run to alert the police!" Ollie yelled.

But before Greta could lock the door, they saw Hans running down the alley and around the corner.

"He's getting away!" Lucy shouted. "I'm going to run after him."

"Don't bother," Ollie said. "Hans' fingerprints are on Mozart's violin. We just have to have the police match the fingerprints to his."

"I wonder why he didn't wear gloves when he switched the violins. That would have kept his fingerprints off the real violin," Lucy said.

"Everyone would have suspected a violinist wearing gloves," Ollie said. "He figured he'd hide the real violin and rub the fingerprints off later."

"Besides, he probably didn't think he'd get caught!" Lottie said.

CHAPTER TWELVE

The kids hiked with Greta Galley through the snow towards the police station. The air was chilly and snowflakes fell in swirls. Lottie danced in a circle, catching snowflakes on her tongue. Lucy tucked the precious violin under her jacket to protect it from the wet snow.

"Weee!" Lottie shouted as she spun fast. "Snow tastes like ice cream!"

"Let me try," Ollie said.

After a moment, they were all dancing down

the sidewalk catching snowflakes on their tongues.

When they got to the police station, Bert Berry and their Dad were waiting outside with Officer Wolf, the police officer they'd met at the museum.

"We found Mozart's violin! It was Hans Avery who stole it," the kids shouted as they ran towards the police station.

Officer Wolf jumped up in surprise.

"Are you sure it was Hans Avery?" he asked.

"One hundred percent sure," Lucy said. "He was running towards the mountains when we last saw him."

Officer Wolf pulled out his walkie-talkie from his police uniform pocket.

"All units please search for Hans Avery. He's the one who switched Mozart's violin with a forgery."

A line of police officers raced out of the building, jumped into their police cars, and sped away with their sirens blaring.

Officer Wolf shook the kids' hands and thanked them for finding the violin. He took Mozart's real violin from Lucy and placed it carefully inside his coat to protect it from the snow.

"How did you ever find the real violin?" He asked.

"I told you, the LOL Detective Club was on the case," Lucy said. "It just took a little sleuthing."

"You've recovered a priceless treasure. The whole country of Austria thanks you," Officer Wolf said. "Well, what are we doing standing in the snow? Please come inside out of the cold, and tell me everything that happened," he continued.

The kids walked into the police station. It was warm and cozy inside and smelled like sugar. Lottie spied a giant chocolate cake in the corner. It was ten layers tall and oozed with chocolate and marshmallow filling.

"Help yourselves to a piece of cake, kids," Officer Wolf said. "Greta Galley was kind enough to bring it for the police officers to share."

"It was for Mozart's birthday party. Because of the violin robbery, it didn't get eaten. It seemed a shame that such a big cake would go to waste," Greta Galley blushed.

"Thank you. Our detective work really worked up an appetite," Lottie smiled.

As the kids ate their slices of birthday cake, the grown-ups began asking them questions.

"I'm so impressed you solved the case! Which one of you figured it out?" Dad asked.

"Well, Ollie videotaped it. That's how we gathered our clues," Lucy said.

"And Lucy figured out that the violins had been switched," Lottie added.

"And if Lottie hadn't played the piano, we never would have known that the violin was hidden inside," Ollie said.

"So, I guess it was a team effort," they all said at the same time.

"Your teamwork really paid off," Officer Wolf smiled.

Lottie cleaned her plate and helped herself to another slice of birthday cake.

"This is delicious," she said with her mouth half full of cake.

"Lottie! Remember your manners," Lucy said.

"Sorry!" Lottie apologized.

Lucy looked at the birthday cake on the table and then at Greta Galley.

"For a moment, I thought that the thief was you, Greta. What were you doing inside the museum?"

"You thought it was me?! What would I ever do with a violin?" Greta laughed. "I went back to get my silver platter. It was my grandmother's platter and I didn't want it to go missing."

"Exactly as I thought!" Lottie exclaimed.

"We went inside to find you, but your bakery was empty. You even locked the front door. Why did you do that?" Lucy asked.

"Oh, I wanted to bring the birthday cake down here for the police to enjoy. So, when I couldn't find you guys, I locked up and dropped off the cake."

Lucy looked over at the cake. It was sitting on top of a shiny, silver platter.

"Your grandmother's platter is beautiful. I can see why you went back to get it," she said.

Just then, Petra Sands walked into the police station. She smiled at the officers, and walked up to Officer Wolf, who was holding the violin.

"Ms. Sands, thank you for coming on such short notice," Officer Wolf said. "The LOL Detective Club has found Mozart's violin. I want you to verify it's the real one."

"It's no problem at all," she said. "Let me take a look at the violin," she said. She examined the violin from the neck to the base.

"Everything looks in order. This is definitely Mozart's violin." She smiled at the kids. "Thank you so much for finding it. My heart was broken when I heard what happened."

"It's the least we could do," Lucy said.

"If you wouldn't mind, Ollie, I would love to get a copy of your video as evidence. If we have that and the fingerprints on the violin, that will be enough to prove Hans Avery switched Mozart's violin for a fake," Officer Wolf said.

"Sure thing," Ollie said. "But, there's one thing that's still bothering me. How did Hans Avery know how to switch the violins? It seems so risky."

"He must have visited the museum many times to craft his plan. I even wonder if he moved the piano closer to the violin's glass case, so it would be easier to switch. I seem to remember the piano being further away from the violin the last time I visited the museum," Petra said.

"But how did he turn off the lights?" Dad asked.

"Oh, I figured that out," Ollie said. "He had a light clicker. It's one of those things you see on TV that turns off lights with a remote control."

"I remember seeing one of those at the train station gift shop," Lottie said.

"Exactly right," Ollie said. "I bet he had one hidden in his pocket. He clicked it and turned off the lights. Then once he'd switched the violins, he clicked it to turn the lights back on."

"Well, the one thing he didn't count on was the LOL Detective Club being on the case. Thanks to your fine detective work, we caught him just in time," Officer Wolf said.

Just then, a big black jeep with spiky tires showed up outside the police station. A driver wearing a ski mask jumped out of the front seat.

"Um, who's that?" Lottie said nervously.

Officer Wolf waved at the man through the

window of the police station.

"Your ride is here," Officer Wolf said to the kids. "I've arranged for you to have ski lessons today up in the mountains. What do you think of that?"

The kids' mouths fell open. "Thank you so much," they cheered.

"It's my way of saying thank you and welcome to Austria," Officer Wolf said.

The kids and their dad jumped inside the warm jeep. A pile of colorful ski jackets and snow boots were in a box in the backseat.

As they drove down the cobblestone street, the wind outside whipped past the jeep's windows, making a high pitched sound.

Lucy giggled to herself.

"What's so funny, Lucy?" Lottie asked.

"I'm just wondering if Mozart's ghost is playing tricks on us again."

The End.

Thank you for reading *LOL Detective Club,
Book #4: The Mozart Mystery!*

Please leave a review on Amazon! I love hearing
what my readers think.

Other Books in the Series:
THE MARDI GRAS MYSTERY:
LOL DETECTIVE CLUB BOOK #1

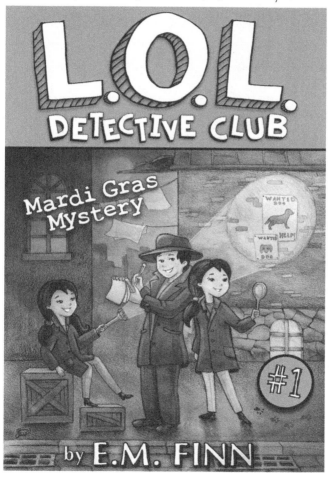

THE PARIS PUZZLER:
LOL DETECTIVE CLUB BOOK #2

CUBNAPPING IN KENYA:
LOL DETECTIVE CLUB BOOK #3

And more coming soon!

About The Author

E.M. Finn writes children's books, including *The LOL Detective Club Mystery Series.*

She lives in Los Angeles with her husband, four daughters, and a Goldendoodle named Daisy.

When she's not writing, she homeschools her children and encourages her husband in his film and television career.

Some of her favorite books include the *Harry Potter* series, *Nancy Drew Mysteries*, *The Boxcar Children*, and the *Little House on the Prairie* books.

Made in the USA
Coppell, TX
19 October 2020

39923937R00059